KU-626-836

B4B 257 515 2   SLS

SCHOOLS LIBRARY SERVICE
MALTBY LIBRARY HEADQUARTERS
HIGH STREET
MALTBY
ROTHERHAM   ‾ ‾ MAY 2005
S66 8LD

Looking
after Little
Ellie

ROTHERHAM LIBRARY & INFORMATION SERVICES

This book must be returned by the date specified at the time of issue
as the DATE DUE FOR RETURN.
The loan may be extended (personally, by post or telephone) for a
further period if the book is not required by another reader, by quoting
the above number / author / title.

LIS7a

For Eleanor, Lizzie, and Andrew

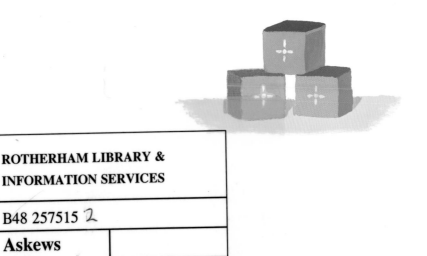

ROTHERHAM LIBRARY & INFORMATION SERVICES	
B48 257515 2	
Askews	
YC	£10.99
	RO 00005510 6

BLOOMSBURY
CHILDREN'S
BOOKS

First published in Great Britain in 2005 by
Bloomsbury Publishing Plc
38 Soho Square, London, W1D 3HB

Text copyright © Dosh Archer 2005
Illustrations copyright © Dosh and Mike Archer 2005
The moral rights of Dosh Archer and Mike Archer to be identified as the
author and illustrators have been asserted
All rights reserved
No part of this publication may be reproduced or transmitted by any means, electronic,
mechanical, photocopying or otherwise, without the prior permission of the publisher

A CIP catalogue record of this book is available from the British Library

ISBN 0 7475 6900 2

Printed and bound in Singapore by Tien Wah Press

1 3 5 7 9 10 8 6 4 2

All papers used by Bloomsbury Publishing are natural, recyclable products made from wood
grown in well-managed forests. The manufacturing processes conform to the
environmental regulations of the country of origin.

Looking After Little Ellie

written and illustrated by
Dosh and Mike Archer

BLOOMSBURY
CHILDREN'S
BOOKS

When Flora rang to ask us to come
and look after Little Ellie,
we said yes.
You have to help your friends.

It was the first time we had
looked after Little Ellie.

Flora said she would be back soon.

But when her mum left,
Little Ellie got a bit upset.

So we did our best to cheer her up.

We gave her
some lunch,

changed her nappy,

and took her to the park.

We played on the swing,

and the see-saw.

We sang for her and danced for her,

and then she had a nap.
She looked really sweet
when she was asleep.

Then it was time to go home.

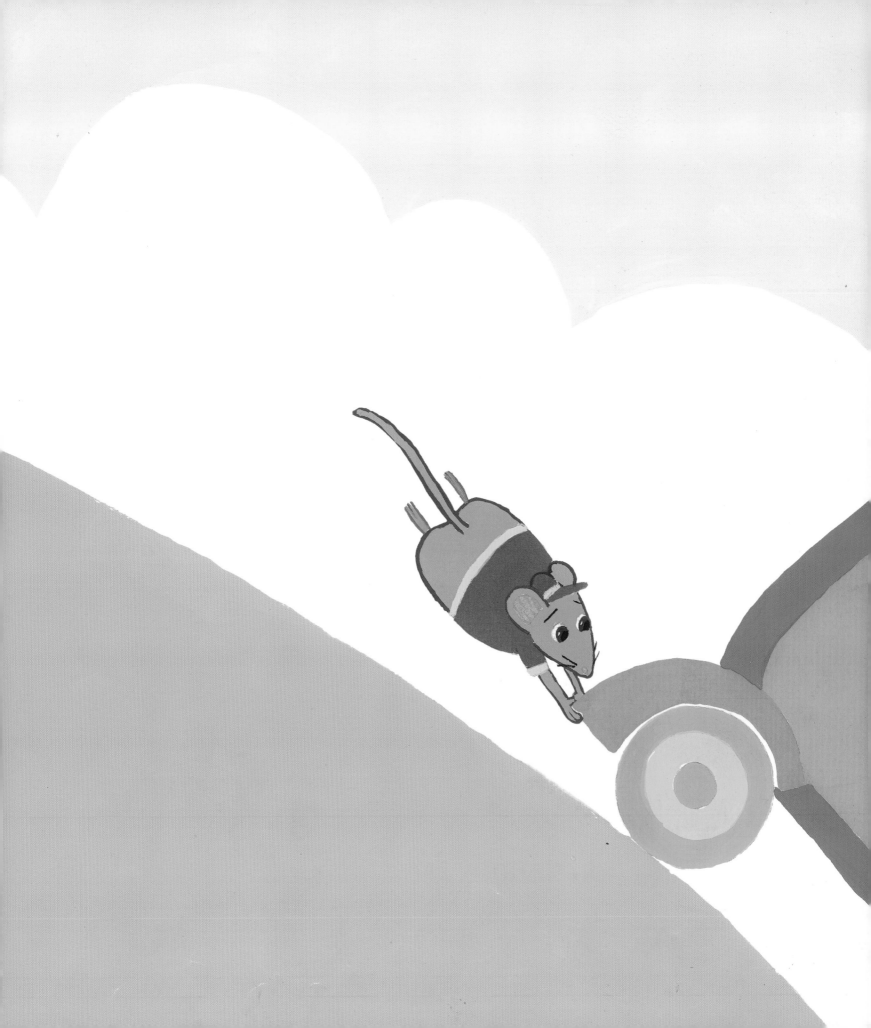

When she got back, Flora said,
'I hope she hasn't been any trouble.'

'Not a bit,' we said,
as we kissed Ellie goodbye.

It's been a big day, but we don't mind.
After all, she's just a little baby.